Sweet Burn

Winter Travers

Copyright © 2018 Winter Travers
All rights reserved. Without limiting the rights under copyright reserved above, no part of this publication may be reproduction, stored in or introduced into a retrieval system, or transmitted, in any form, or by any means (electronic, mechanical, photocopying, recording, or otherwise) utilization of this work without written permission of both the copyright owner and the above publisher of this book.
This is a work of fiction. Names, characters, places, brands, media and incidents are either the products of the author's imagination or are used fictitiously. The author acknowledges the trademarked status and trademark owners of various products referenced in this work of fiction, which have been used without permission. The publication/use of these trademarks is not authorized, associated with, or sponsored by the trademark owners.

For questions or comments about this book, please contact the author at wintertravers84@gmail.com

Also by Winter Travers

Devil's Knights Series:
Loving Lo
Finding Cyn
Gravel's Road
Battling Troy
Gambler's Longshot
Keeping Meg
Fighting Demon
Unraveling Fayth

Skid Row Kings Series:
DownShift
PowerShift
BangShift

Fallen Lords MC Series
Nickel
Pipe
Maniac
Wrecker

Powerhouse MA Series
Dropkick My Heart
Love on the Mat
Black Belt in Love
Black Belt Knockout

Nitro Crew Series
Burndown
Holeshot (September 29th)

Table of Contents

Chapter 1
Chapter 2
Chapter 3
Chapter 4
Chapter 5
Chapter 6
First Chapter of Loving Lo
First Chapter of Downshift
First Chapter of Dropkick My Heart
First Chapter of Burndown

Chapter 1

Brynn

"Do you have the order for Lackwitz?"

"The who?"

"Lackwitz?"

Karen buried her head in the weekly planner. "Hmm, I'm not seeing it. Can you say it one more time for me?"

"Lackwitz. I think that they ordered the-"

Karen burst out laughing. "I heard you the first time, Brynn, I just think it's hilarious to hear you say it."

I flipped her the bird. "You're a bitch. Now tell me what they ordered so I can add it to the bake list for tomorrow."

She flipped through the book. "Two tiered anniversary cake. Chocolate cake, mint mousse filling, orange/blue."

I scoffed. "Orange and blue? Lord have mercy." Sometimes I wished I had free reign with these orders. Blue and orange were meant for birthdays, not anniversaries.

"Those were their wedding colors ten years ago. She was very insistent on having them on the cake," Karen explained.

I sighed and added the cake to the bake list. "Well, I guess that's what she'll get then."

The bell out front dinged. "You want me to get that?"

"No." I waved her off. "I know you have to get going. We have the schedule ready for tomorrow, so you're good."

Karen took off her apron, and tossed it in the hamper. "You manning the front counter. This is a change."

That was the truth. I had Karen so I never had to step foot out front and I was left to bake and create. "With five minutes left in the day, I think I can handle it." The bell rang again. "I hope."

Karen grabbed her bag and laughed. "Good luck, girl. You got this," she laughed before ducking out.

I tucked my pencil behind my ear and straightened my apron. "Coming!" I called as I pushed through the swinging door.

Three firefighters were standing in front of the dessert case.

"Whoa. No Karen today?" The shorter one asked.

"She's gone for the day. You're stuck with me." I held up my hands and shrugged. Who knew Karen had such a following?

"She okay?" The one with shaggy hair asked.

"Just had an appointment. But I'll make sure to let her know her fan club stopped by." I laughed and grabbed a pair of rubber gloves from the back counter.

"I think I'm okay with Karen being gone for the day."

I pulled on my gloves and looked up into the greenest eyes I had ever seen. "Uh, um ... Karen?" Putting together a single thought was a problem for me right then, let alone remembering what he had asked.

He chuckled, and leaned against the case. "Is this your first day, honey?"

My eyes fluttered, and the ability to think slowly came back to me. "First day?"

The three guys laughed.

"We're just used to seeing Karen whenever we come in," Shorty explained.

I cleared my throat, and put my hands on the counter. Pull it together, Brynn. "I work in the back."

"So you're responsible for all of this goodness?" Green eyes asked.

"Um, yeah. I made all of this." And own all of this. I felt like a five year old boosting they had colored a picture.

"Impressive." He nodded his head and looked over everything in the case.

It was impressive. I worked my ass off everyday starting at three in the morning to overfill the case. At this time of the day most everything was gone, except for a few of this and that. "Um, was there anything you guys were wanting?"

"We'll take everything left."

My eyes bugged out. While the things in the case were dwindling, there were still at least twenty different things in there. Jelly donuts, half a dozen cupcakes, two small cakes, and a handful of cookies and pastries. "Erg, everything?" The two small cakes could at least feed ten people.

"Yeah. It's Abe's turn to cook, and instead of actually cooking, he just likes to buy everything and pass it off as his own." Shorty seemed to be the talker of the group. Not afraid to say what was on his mind. Definitely not the type of personality I was drawn to. This was exactly why I tended to stick to the kitchen.

"And you assholes don't seem to complain when I do it."

"Well, when you get lasagna from Mario's and dessert from Maggie Mays, yeah, we aren't going to complain." The guys laughed and Shorty put his hand on the counter by the cash register. "Fill the boxes, boss lady."

I empty the leftover pastries and things into two boxes, and put the two cakes in clear plastic containers. "Um, that'll be it?" I asked.

Green eyes looked around. "You got anything else back there for me?"

My cheeks heated, and my eyes wildly looked around. Was he hitting on me? Was he looking for more cupcakes? Did he want *my* cupcakes?

A loud, shrill, beeping noise went off and each guy grabbed their walkie talkie things they had strapped to their chests.

Shorty and Shaggy took off out the door, hollering they would be in the truck.

"No time to add all of this up." He slapped a hundred dollar bill down on the counter. "This cover it?"

I nodded dumbly. "More than enough."

He grabbed the box and two containers of cake, and hightailed it out the door. "Later, Sweets."

I grabbed the hundred and put it in the cash register. What he had bought was around forty dollars. My baking was good, but it wasn't worth a sixty dollar tip.

I moved to the window to watch the fire truck roll by with its lights and sirens on. Mark's Corners was sprawled on the door with Station Number Two underneath it.

Green eyes had payed me way too much, and I was going to make sure he got his change tomorrow. I still had a couple hours of prep in front of me for tomorrow, and I had just added a few extra things to my list for a certain fire department.

*

Chapter 2

Abe

"You wanna tell me what the hell that shit was? I told you I had point, and you still went in there guns blazing."

O'Donnell shook his head. "I had assessed the situation, Capt. I knew what I was doing."

Captain Douglas took his hat off, and tossed it on the floor. "Is that what you want me to tell your family when we pull you out of the rubble? You assessed the situation? Your assessment was way off," he shouted.

I cleared my throat. "With all due respect, Sir, I would have done the same thing had I been in his shoes."

Capt. clapped his hands together. "Well, thank god. Abe to the fucking rescue. Again. Both of you get out of here, and try not to fuck up anymore, got me?"

I pushed O'Donnell out the door and down the hallway.

Capt. slammed the door behind us, and I tried not to laugh as he continued to rant to his empty office.

"I don't know why he's so pissed. It's not like it was that bad. It was just a little smoke coming out of the roof." O'Donnell collapsed onto the couch in the living area of the firehouse.

"Probably because you didn't follow protocol." I grabbed two bottles of water from the fridge, and tossed one to O'Donnell. We had just gotten back from the call on

Elm and Twelfth and were greeted to an ass ripping by the Captain.

"Dude, fuck protocol. Ain't no damn reason why I shouldn't have done what I did."

I agreed with him to an extent. Yes, this time it didn't really matter that O'Donnell went in without a cover, but next time he might not be so lucky. "Dude, is it really that hard for you to just chill out and wait for someone to have your back?"

He glared at me. "Do I get a lecture from you now, too?"

I held up my hands. "Pretty sure I just had to go through that same lecture, since I was the dumbass who followed you in."

He twisted the cap off his bottle, and tossed it on the battered coffee table. "That's because you didn't follow protocol right behind me."

"I was making sure you didn't get your ass killed."

"When is dinner being delivered?" Anderson walked into the kitchen, and eyed the pink box in front of me. "Is that dinner?"

I grabbed the box and pulled it close. "No, dumbass. Dinner should be here in ten minutes. I called Mario's on the way back from the call."

"Thank, god. I think my stomach is starting to eat itself." Anderson pulled out a chair at the island bar, and held out his hand. "Give me a cupcake or something."

I shook my head. "Not happening, brother. I open this box, and everything will be gone before the lasagna even gets here."

He pointed a finger at me. "I know for a fact you got more than enough food for tonight. Either give me a cupcake, or start slicing one of those cakes you got hiding in the fridge."

"I don't know if I'd be demanding one of his cupcakes, Anderson. I think Abe is fond of those cupcakes," O'Donnell taunted.

Anderson rubbed his chin. "You know, he did seem rather fond of that baker chick today."

"Don't know what either of you idiots are talking about." I flipped open the top of the box, and pushed it forward. "Have at it."

Anderson and O'Donnell looked at each other. "Nope," they said in unison.

"You bitch about needing a fucking cupcake, and now that I offer you one, you say no?" What the hell was up with these guys?

"You get the chick's name?" Anderson asked.

"What chick?"

"Your mother." O'Donnell rolled his eyes. "The cake chick, dumbass."

I shut the box, and set it on the back counter. "Nah."

"Nah is all he's got to say," Anderson chuckled. "If you're not interested, then I think maybe I'll head back over to the bakery tomorrow and see about her cupcakes."

Even Anderson couldn't keep a straight face.

O'Donnell busted out laughing, and I shook my head.

"That the line you gonna hand her?" I asked.

"Better than any shit you would try to say."

"Yo, Brickley, food is here," one of the guys hollered.

Anderson shook his head. "Saved by the food," he mumbled. "When your ass gets back up here, you can tell me how you'd woo the bakery chick."

I shook my head, and jogged down the stairs to the waiting delivery guy. "Hey, Mikey. Perfect timing." I forked over two hundred dollar bills, and grabbed the three overflowing bags filled with breadsticks, lasagna, and ziti.

"Mario's appreciates you guys." He tucked the bills into his pocket. "Need help taking it up?"

"Nope, all good, Mikey. See you in two weeks."

He shook his head, and slipped out the door.

"Dinner," I yelled to the guys who were cleaning the truck from the last call. They would be up in seconds since they all knew it was Mario's for dinner tonight.

Anderson and O'Donnell each grabbed a bag from me after I climbed the stairs, and started spreading everything out on the long table. There were always ten guys on shift, and we could put away two pans of lasagna easily.

"So, you gonna ask her out?" Anderson took the lid off the pan of ziti, and tossed it in the trash.

"Why are you so interested in who I may or may not ask out?" Dude was worse than my mother wondering when I was going to settle down and have kids.

He shrugged and grabbed a breadstick. "I was thinking if you date her, you can put a good word in for me with Karen."

I threw my head back and laughed. "You're giving me shit, asking when I'm gonna ask her out when you can't even ask her friend out." Typical Anderson. All talk and no action.

"Brother, have you seen Karen? She's way out of my league."

I had seen her, and while I agreed with Anderson that she was out of his league, he could still get her. "I'm not your matchmaker, dingleberry. Ask her out on your own."

He shoved the breadstick in his mouth. "Loff a gaud ew argh."

"Try that without your mouth full."

He gulped and shook his head. "A lot of good you are."

I clapped him on the shoulder. "You're gonna have to do this one on your own, brother."

"That mean you aren't going to ask cupcake chick out?"

I laughed. "That doesn't have anything to do with you."

"Got it, got it," he mumbled.

Anderson knew I didn't like to talk about my personal life. Most of these guys knew the bare minimum, and they only found that shit out after years of knowing me. "Go grab some food, brother, and try to grow some balls to ask Karen out."

He flipped me off and grabbed a plate off the table. "Easier said than done," he grumbled.

A lot of things were easier said than done, but that was what made them worthwhile.

While I had every intention of going back to the bakery to find out the shy, brunette's name, Anderson didn't need to know that.

*

Chapter 3

Brynn

"Here."

"What?"

"You take it."

Karen set down the box. "Um, I'm not the one who decided to make them a cake." She pointed to the box. "A big ass cake, by the way."

"It's not that big."

"A half sheet cake filled with cherry amaretto is big, and delicious."

Well, delicious is what I strived for. Who cares if it was on the larger side? "He gave me a hundred dollars, Karen. I barely gave him fifty dollars worth of day old pastries and cakes."

"They come in every other week. I can give him his change then."

I looked down at the floor and sighed. She was right. I didn't need to take the cake to them, but now I had made the dang thing, and I didn't want it to go to waste.

"How about I go over there with you?"

Thank god for Karen taking mercy on me. "Really?"

She shook her head. "Yes. I leave you alone for one day to close up, and we're taking field trips to the fire station."

"Five minutes. We drop it off, we leave."

She untied her apron, and tossed it in the laundry basket. "You're doing all of the talking. I'm on the lookout for a sexy firefighter boyfriend."

"I'm sure you'll be able to walk out with one in five minutes."

She scoffed and untied her long hair from the top of her head. "Doubtful. I've had my eye on one for months, and he never talks to me."

Oh shoot. Maybe the guy she likes was green eyes. "Oh, does he always come in?" *Please don't let it be green eyes, please.*

"He's really not my normal type, but he's got longer sandy blonde hair, that kind of falls in his eyes, and each time he shakes his head to get it out of his eyes, I swoon a little bit." She fanned her face with her hand, and leaned against the counter.

Well thank goodness she wasn't swooning over green eyes. There was no way in hell I would be able to compete for a man against Karen. She was tall, slim, and had gorgeous long, flowy blonde hair. She was a goddess, plain and simple.

"I think he was in here yesterday. Super cute, Karen." He was, but just not my type. I was more into the tall, dark, handsome green eyes. "Do you happen to know the guys names?"

She smirked. "You have your eye the tall one, don't you?"

I shook my head. Deny, deny, deny. "No."

"I know you, Brynn. That man is handsome, and I know he's the one who paid, because he always does."

I grabbed the box. "We should get this over to the fire station."

She giggled, and grabbed her purse from under the cabinet. "I'll drive, and you can tell me how Brynn Marshall has finally looked over her mixing bowl and noticed a man."

I rolled my eyes and followed her out the front door to her car that was parked on the curb. "You should really leave the good parking spots for the customers," I called as I slid into the front seat with the cake in my hands.

Karen jogged around the front of the car. "You're acting like I took every parking spot on the block, Brynn." She slid into the driver's seat, and started the car. She glanced over at me and smiled. "You look like you're about to barf."

I leaned my head back and sighed. "Why am I doing this?" *Because last night all you could dream about was the green eyed man.*

"Cause you like him," Karen sang. She shifted the car into drive, and merged into traffic. "And, you're too nice of a person to accept a fifty dollar tip. While I would have taken it, and put it towards my Coach bag fund."

"Do you know where we are going?"

"Station Two."

I bet she didn't have to peek out the window to figure that out. Where Karen was outgoing and confident, I was stuck back by the ovens praying no one noticed me. My eyes closed and I counted to thirty. Then I counted to twenty.

"We're here."

I cracked open an eye, and looked up at Station Two of Mark's Corners. "Can we just leave it on the front stoop?"

Karen laughed. "No. You and I are prancing our happy asses into the station, and giving these guys the best cake they'll ever taste."

"It'll still taste amazing if we leave it at the front door."

"Come on, Marshall. It's time to see if your prince charming is working today."

I sat up. "Wait, you mean he might not be working today?" Maybe this wouldn't be as bad as I had made it out to be in my head. Maybe I was worried for nothing?

Karen got out of the car. She walked around the front, and opened my door. "Only one way to find out." She swept her arm out, and bowed.

Lord have mercy. "It's about damn time you curtsy."

Karen straightened, and slammed the door shut behind me. "I was bowing to the cake. I'm hoping these guys decide to cut the cake before we leave so I can snag a piece."

"The fact you love my cake is reassuring." She jogged a few steps to get in front of me, and opened the door to the fire station.

"Best cake within one hundred miles, Brynn," she whispered as I walked by. "You got this."

I rolled my eyes, and looked around. I had thought that we would have walked into a reception area or something, but instead we had walked in where the huge fire trucks lived. "Sweet Jesus," I gasped.

"You totally should have put a fire truck or a dog on that cake."

I looked over at Karen. What the hell was she talking about? "Dog?"

"Dalmatian," she clarified.

That made more sense. "Where do you think we go?"

She tapped chin and looked around. "You would think there would be a firefighting badass room."

Dear god. This was a horrible idea. I was standing here with a big ass cake in my arms, and Karen was looking for the badass firefighter room. We were a pair of nuts.

"Can I help you ladies?"

We both spun around and were face to face with Shorty.

"Cal!" Karen shouted.

I looked him up and down. Shorty fit him better.

"Karen? What are you doing here?" he asked.

She hitched her thumb at me. "Brynn got you guys some goodies yesterday, and Abe tipped her too much. She brought over a cake to make up for it."

Cal rubbed his stomach. "Now that sounds amazing. We had the last of the cake from yesterday for breakfast."

I wrinkled my nose. "For breakfast?" I was all for cake, but I much prefer a donut for breakfast than cake.

"Yeah. It's really amazing it made it that long. You want me to go get Abe for you?" Cal motioned up the staircase to the right.

"No."

"Yes," we both said at the same time.

Karen glared at me. "Yes, we'd love it if you could get him."

Cal jogged up the stairs.

"That's totally the badass firefighter lair up there." She moved to the stairs, and looked up them. "It's just stairs," she whispered.

"What the hell did you think it was going to be?" I hissed. "A stairway to top-less firefighters and Dalmatians?"

She wiggled her eyebrows. "Now that would definitely be a stairway to heaven."

"Do you inhale the overspray while I'm airbrushing? Is that what's wrong with you? Has it all gone to your brain?"

She stuck her tongue out and crossed her eyes. "No, I just eat icing by the spoonful."

A sugar high. That would explain her kooky behavior.

"Someone's coming." She scurried away from the stairs, and stood behind me.

"What are you doing?" I whispered. I spun to face her, but she grabbed onto my shoulders, and moved whenever I did. "Dammit, Karen. What the hell?" We spun around three times with her basically attached to my shoulders, but I couldn't see her face to face.

A low, masculine voice sounded behind us. "Uh, were you ladies looking for me?"

I stopped spinning, and my eyes bugged up. "Please tell me that isn't him," I whispered to Karen.

"Uh, it's not him?"

Yeah, that sounded convincing. Here I was, spinning around like a dog chasing it's tail with Karen clinging to my back.

Perfect first impression. Well, second impression.

"Uh, well..." I stuttered. All thought left my mind and I was wondering what exactly were words, and how I could string them together to make a coherent thought.

"We were just testing out some new boxes that Brynn got in. It's so hard to find a sturdy box these days." Karen steered me around to face green eyes.

Damn.

He was sexy.

I thrusted the box at him. "Cake." Just call me Brynn the cavewoman. Oh oh ah, here cake. All I needed to do was beat on my chest, and the transformation would be complete.

"You brought me a cake?"

He seemed to be ignoring my inner cavewoman. *There was a god.* "Um, yeah. You paid me way too much yesterday, and I felt bad."

He shook his head. "You didn't have to do this." He lifted the lid off the cake, and he closed his eyes as he inhaled deeply. "Holy crap."

"Is that cake? Fuck you, that is a cake." It sounded like a herd of elephants were marching down the stars.

Shaggy came to a skidding stop next to green eyes, and put his hands on the box. "Cake," he moaned.

Green eyes elbowed him in the gut, and motioned to Karen and I. "Guests, you dumbass."

Shaggy straightened up, and his jaw dropped when he looked at Karen and I. "Whoa. Today just became a phenomenal day." A huge grin spread across his lips, and he didn't take his eyes off Karen. It looked like the feeling was mutual between the two.

Karen laughed, and elbowed me in the side. "Brynn thought she needed to bring a cake over. I tagged along. I've never been in a fire station before."

Shaggy cleared his throat. "You want me to give you the two cent tour?"

Karen batted her eyes, and fluffed her hair. "That would be awesome." She grabbed the arm he gallantly offered, and wrapped her hand around his bicep. "You can take care of Brynn, right, Abe?"

"Uh, yeah. You guys take your time." Karen and Shaggy took off into the large garage and I was left alone with green eyes.

My idea of bringing Karen along had backfired since she had abandoned her post as my wing woman. I needed to find something to say, and I needed to figure it out now. "So, uh, I wasn't sure if you were going to be working." I would have slapped myself on the forehead if he wouldn't have thought that I was an idiot.

"I'm in the middle of a four on. Friday at eight am I'm off for three days."

"Wow. Four days in a row?"

"Yeah.

"Twenty four hours a day?" That sounded insane to me.

He chuckled. "Yeah. That's how it goes."

While I was at the bakery a lot, it wasn't like I was saving lives or risking my life with every cake I put in the oven. "Impressive."

"Uh, did you want your own tour of the fire house?"

I looked around. "Um, if you're not too busy. I don't want to take you away from something important."

He motioned up the stairs. "How about we take this upstairs, and we can start the tour up there. Right now that's the most important thing I have to do."

My cheeks heated at his words. "Well, then I'd love a tour."

He moved up the stairs, and my eyes were trained on his tight butt that I wanted to squeeze and see if it was as firm as it looked.

"Up here is where we do most of our relaxing when we have down time from calls."

Concentrate, Brynn. "Um, do you guys have much down time?"

He shrugged his shoulders and stood at the top of the steps waiting for me. "It really goes in spurts. Some days we'll get ten calls, and then other days we barely get two."

"But less calls is a good thing, right?"

He smiled. "Yeah, sweetheart. Definitely a good thing." He motioned to the left. "We'll go this way first.

Here we have the kitchen and living area where you can normally find a few guys."

The kitchen was huge. The ceilings were all vaulted opening up the space, and there were several yards of counter space with cabinets beneath them. The oven and stove were twice the size of anything you would see in a house, with a huge hood hung over the stove top. There were two dishwashers, a large sink, and various kitchen appliances littered over the counter tops.

"Wow. This is amazing." You know those home shows of people looking to buy a new house, and they tour three or four houses? I love watching them just to see the kitchen. I am a kitchen whore. Big, small, or in between, I love to look at them.

"Yeah, it's good for the guys who like to cook?"

"And that's not you," I laughed.

He shook his head. "Um, yeah. Not me at all. In my thirty-four years of life I've discovered I'm not intended to be in the kitchen."

"Good thing you have delicious restaurants and bakeries in Mark's Corners to help you out then."

"Right on, sweetheart." He placed his hand on the small of my back, and guided me through the kitchen and into a dining room that opened up to a large living room that had a pool table, and an air hockey table along with two large sectionals in front of a ginormous TV.

"I don't think your TV is big enough…" I turned to look at him. "I still don't know what your name is."

"Abe, sweetheart. You're Brynn, right?"

I nodded my head. "Yup, that's me."

His eyes warmed to a dark green, and he smiled down at me. "It suits you."

Um, huh? "Thank you?"

"It's as pretty as you are." He guided me back the way we came to the other side of the stairs.

"Do you guys have paramedics here?"

"Yeah? Everything okay?" His voice was filled with concern.

"I'm good, but I think you must have bumped your head before I got here. You should really get that checked out."

He shook his head and chuckled. "Haven't bumped my head all day. Just call them like I see them." He swept out his hand. "This is where we sleep."

There were fifteen beds spread out in the large room, with three of the beds occupied by sleeping bodies. "It's like summer camp," I whispered.

Abe chuckled, and grabbed my hand. "That's a good assessment, except no mosquitoes."

He pulled me out of the community bedroom, and into the small hallway by the stairs.

I looked around. "Okay. Now where is the fire pole?"

"That might be a myth, sweetheart. I've never had a fire pole in any of the firehouses I've worked in."

I pouted out my bottom lip. "Well, that's a bit disappointing." Not that I would have actually slid down the thing, but I would have loved to watch Abe do it.

"Whoa. More cake?"

"Sounds like the guys found the cake you brought over."

I leaned forward and looked into the kitchen. "Well, I did bring it for you guys, so I guess that's a good thing."

"It'll be gone before morning."

"Um, well, I better get going so you can grab a slice before it's all gone."

He tightened his grip on my hand, and leaned into me. "Don't go yet."

I looked up into his mesmerizing green eyes. "Um, I need to get back to the bakery to get everything ready for tomorrow." Waking up at four am was easier when I knew that everything was ready for me.

"Well, what are you doing tomorrow night?"

"Tomorrow?" I squeaked out.

"Yeah."

"Um." Tomorrow was Friday night, also known as the night I binge watched the latest Netflix series and ate a pint of ice cream. "I tend to stay in."

"Well, how about you come out with me? I know of a great little place I'd love to take you to."

Erg, me? "I … uh … well."

"She'd love to." Karen stood in the entry to the kitchen with a plate of cake in her hand. "She lives above the bakery. You can pick her up at seven."

"Wait, what? How could you-," I sputtered. Whose side was she on?

"You okay with that, Brynn?"

I looked up into his eyes and sighed. Who was I kidding? I should be thanking Karen up and down for jumping in, and saying yes for me. If I had been alone I would have made up some lame excuse and spent Friday night alone like I always do. "Um, that should be fine."

He squeezed my hand, and a panty dropping smile spread across his lips. Lord have mercy, this man should be illegal. "I'll see you tomorrow night, sweetheart."

"'Kay." Yup, that was the only thing I managed to say. My brain was complete mush just by one touch from Abe.

"Later, Karen." Abe walked into the kitchen, and I collapsed against the wall.

"No time for that right now." Karen looped her arm through mine, and pulled me down the stairs. "We can swoon over Abe and Blake in the car."

"Blake?"

She bound down the last three steps, and pushed open the door. "Shaggy."

"Did we both just get dates?"

Karen beeped open the locks on her car, and looked over her shoulder at me. "We sure did, and you are not canceling yours."

I slid into the car, and looked up at the fire station. As of right now I had no plans to cancel on Abe. I didn't have his phone number or any way to get in touch with him, so it really wasn't an option to cancel.

I wasn't sure if that was a good thing or not.

*

Chapter 4

Abe

I knocked.
And waited.
Knocked again.
And waited.

It was two minutes to seven and I was wondering if Brynn was ever going to open the door. "Brynn, sweetheart?"

I heard a scuffle behind the door, and the lock on the door finally turned. She pulled open the door, and looked down at the floor. "Hey."

You wanna know what I didn't understand? Women who were drop dead gorgeous and were shy as hell. Brynn was the most beautiful woman I had ever met. "Up here, Brynn." I reached out, and put a finger under her chin. "Let me see those pretty eyes."

She tipped back her head, and tucked her hair behind her ear. "Not as pretty as yours."

A smirk spread across my lips. "You think I'm pretty?"

"Erg, not pretty, but pretty for a man."

"You still called me pretty, sweetheart." She moved to shut the door, and I put my foot out to stop her. "What are you doing?"

"Starting over. I really can't go on this date with me calling you pretty." She looked expectantly at me to move my foot.

I held up my hands, and stepped back. Odd, but if that's what she wanted, she could have it. I stared at the closed door waiting for her to open it.

"Knock," she called through the door.

I shook my head, and raised my hand to knock. "Kooky."

She opened the door and smiled. "Hi, Abe."

Okay, she was right, that was much better. "Hey, sweetheart." I moved in, resting my hand on her waist, and pressed a kiss to the side of her head. "You look beautiful."

She blushed under my words, and a light sigh left her lips. "So do you." She winced, and threw her hands in the air. "Dang it. Now I called you beautiful." She started to close to door, and I put my arm out.

"Nope, not again, sweetheart. Sometimes you just gotta take what you're given, and move on." I pushed my way into her apartment, and shut the door behind me. She only got one redo. I could accept the fact she had called me beautiful. Funny, but I accepted it. "What's that smell?"

Her cheeks heated again. "Uh, well, I was just working on something."

My mouth watered at the heavenly smell. "Do I get to be your taste tester?"

She glanced over her shoulder into the small kitchen. "Uh, it's not ready yet. I literally just took it out of the oven when you knocked the first time."

"What is it?" I had never smelled something so delicious before.

"Double chocolate bundt cake. Once it cools I plan to put a salted caramel drizzle on it."

Sweet heaven above, chocolate and caramel. I ran my fingers through my hair. "Any chance you know when it's going to be done?"

She laughed. "About an hour."

That was perfect. "You ready for dinner?" If we ate now, we could be back to have cake for dessert.

"Yeah." She grabbed her purse, and hitched it over her shoulder.

I eyed the cake sitting on the counter. "You sure it'll be okay while we're gone?"

She threw her head back and laughed. "You're concern for the cake is nice, but it'll be okay by itself. It won't throw a rager or anything like that."

"You sure? Maybe we should bring it with us." She giggled and I watched.

Damn, Brynn was beautiful. Her long, brunette hair flowed around her shoulders as her blue eyes lit up. I wasn't going to be able to keep my hands off of her.

My hand rested on her hip, and I pulled her close to me. She rested her hand on my chest, and her laughter died. "Abe," she breathed out.

"You looked so beautiful, sweetheart, I needed to see it up close."

Pink climbed her cheeks, and she ducked her head into my shoulder.

My hand slid around her waist, and pulled her close. "Don't be embarrassed, sweetheart."

She looked up at me. "I'm not embarrassed, it's just no one has ever said anything like that to me."

That was going to change as long as I was around.

*

Brynn

This had never happened before.

The man barely knew me, and I was in his arms while he told me how beautiful I was.

All of my past relationships were blah and mediocre. I wasn't even in a relationship with Abe, and he was already treating me better.

"You really wanna go out tonight?"

I blinked slowly. Maybe I was reading this whole thing wrong. "Uh, I guess if you don't want to go out—"

He shook his head. "Brynn, I still want to go on a date with you, I just mean do we have to leave, or can we just stay here?"

Oh. That was good. "Um, I could cook?"

"Only if you want, or we could order something in."

I smiled. "I did hear that was your specialty, but I think I can wrangle something up for us. We just might have to run to the store around the corner for a few things."

"I like the sound of that."

"Just let me take a peek in the fridge, make a list, and then we can go, yeah?"

He nodded his head. "Sounds like a good plan, sweetheart."

I rummaged through the fridge knowing I had most everything I needed to make spaghetti. All we were going to have to pick up was hamburger, Italian sausage, and garlic. And wine. Lots of wine. I was two seconds away from freaking out about Abe being in my kitchen.

He was hovering by the bundt cake, watching me.

"Um, we just need a couple of things. Plus I can grab a loaf of bread from the bakery."

"You even make bread? Holy hell, woman."

I shrugged. "Um, yeah?"

"Incredible," he muttered.

It really wasn't. Compared to the bakeries I had worked at in the past, I didn't make much. I was a one woman bakery with Karen manning the front.

We made a quick dash to the store with Abe insisting on paying for everything. He carried the bags on the way back, and even held my hand.

I felt like a blushing school girl when his fingers had intertwined with mine. He led me up the stairs, unpacked the bags, and sat at the kitchen table while I cooked.

"You really don't know how to cook?" I leaned against the stove next to the counter, and picked up my wine glass.

"It's not for a lack of trying." He leaned back in his chair. "Growing up my meals were always cooked for me, and by the time I moved out, I tried to cook, but I'm just not meant to do more than use a microwave and toaster."

"How did you live till your twenties with someone always making your meals for you?" I wished I had that. By the time I was thirteen I had discovered that I was a better cook than my mom, and we both agreed that I would cook.

"Uh, well, we had a cook."

I smiled. "So did we. It was me." I wiggled my eyebrows. I stirred the sauce in the pan. Abe was quiet, and I wasn't sure what had just happened. "So, what kind of food do you survive on now?"

Abe cleared his throat. "Can we go back to me telling you we had a cook growing up?"

I shrugged. "If you want to. Although, I must say it's pretty damn cool."

"I've never told anyone that. At least not since I moved to Mark's Corners over ten years ago."

"I guess I should feel honored then," I laughed nervously.

"I wanna tell you everything, sweetheart."

"Maybe we should save everything for the second date?" I was just getting used to the man being in my kitchen. Perhaps we could save the soul bearing talk for another time.

He chuckled. "I don't have hideous secrets. I've just never told anyone about the real me. I tend to stick to the surface details."

"Well, I guess that's reassuring." I cleared my throat unsure of what to say next. I drained the last of my wine, and set the glass down. "Did you want more?"

Abe stood up and grabbed the bottle from the table. "I got you." He filled my glass to the top, and topping off his own. He leaned against the counter, and grabbed my hand. "Did I scare you away?"

"I'd be lying if I said I was fine, but I'm not scared away. Just a bit taken back." No one had ever wanted to tell me everything. Didn't everyone have secrets? Whether they were small or big, we all had them.

He pulled me over, and positioned me in front of him, standing between his legs. "Good. I didn't want to have to leave before we had dinner."

"Or cake," I added.

He nodded. "Definitely not before cake."

"What are we doing, Abe?"

He rested his hands on my waist. "Getting to know each other. Finding out if we want to spend more time together."

"Uh, so what's the consensus so far?" I knew where my head was, but I had to wonder what he was thinking. Was this one night? A couple of nights?

"I like you. I knew I liked you the other day in the bakery."

"Pretty sure I spoke maybe ten words, and most of them didn't make sense." I cringed just thinking about it.

"You were damn adorable."

"That's exactly what every grown woman wants to hear. Adorable." I stuck my tongue out.

"Now, now, sweetheart. I also thought your ass looked amazing when you turned around."

I slugged him on the shoulder. "You're such a man."

"Pretty sure that's one of the main things you like about me."

The water boiled over on the pasta, and I pulled away from Abe. "You may be on to something." Being a man was on the list of things I liked about Abe. I mean, if he were a girl, I wouldn't be cooking him spaghetti in my apartment right now. I tested the noodles, and dumped them into the colander. "You ready to eat?" I pulled the garlic bread out of the oven, and slid it onto a plate.

"I'm starving."

He helped set the table, and I laid the sauce, noodles, and bread in the center of the table.

"You forgot the cake."

I rolled my eyes, and grabbed the cake. "You're making me think you are here only for the cake."

We sat down, and filled our plates.

"Gotta tell you. You make the best cake I've ever had in my life. So, yeah, knowing you made a cake is fucking amazing. Add on the fact I don't need to share it with any of those fuckers at the fire station makes it even more amazing."

I twirled some noodles around my fork. "How long exactly have you been buying out the case in the bakery?"

He wiped his mouth with his napkin, and took a sip of wine. "Um, for about a year."

Holy crap. He had been coming to the bakery, my bakery, every other week for a year, and I had no idea. "Seriously?" I really needed to get out of the back.

"Yeah, and for that whole year Karen and Anderson have been dancing around each other. It was about time he got off the pot and asked her out."

"So he's a good guy?"

"One of the best I know."

That was reassuring to know. Karen was on a date with him right now, so hopefully she wouldn't be calling me later crying about what a dick he was.

"How did you get into making amazing cakes?"

Hmm, I guess it was question time. I took a bite. "Well, I've been cooking and baking since I was ten, and by the time I turned thirteen, I was doing all of the cooking. It was only natural that my first job was a dishwasher at the local diner."

"Ren's on fifth?"

I nodded. "Yup. Ren's mom was the one who took me under her wing, and taught me all her baking secrets."

"I'll have to stop in and thank her, although I have to think you're just a natural when it comes to the kitchen. This spaghetti rivals Mario's."

I blushed under his praise. "I think you might want to slow down on the wine."

He chuckled and shook his head. "I just know good food when I eat it, sweetheart."

"Now it's your turn to tell me how you became a firefighter." Time to turn the tables on him. "How does a man with a personal chef become a public servant?"

"Now you're just making it sound a bit dramatic. I wasn't the crowned prince of a country or anything."

We ate in silence for a bit while he gathered his thoughts.

I finished most of my food, and pushed back the plate. "I'm waiting for my story, Abe. No cake until you spill."

"I thought you weren't ready for everything?"

I shrugged, and swirled the wine in my glass. "We'll call it getting to know each other."

"It's not some grand story, sweetheart. I wanted a job where I felt needed."

"What did you do before?"

"I worked for my father."

Hmm, now we were getting somewhere, but it was like pulling teeth. "So, what does your father do?"

"He owned a few businesses, and I managed one for him. He passed away, and my mother and I decided it was best to sell them off."

"I'm sorry, Abe." That took a turn I wasn't expecting.

He shrugged. "My father was a hard man to work with. While he provided a good life for me growing up, he expected things from my mother and I that were hard to fulfill."

"You mom lives here?"

"No." He shook his head. "She lives in California in the house I grew up in. I've tried to get her to move to Mark's Corners, but she likes the warm weather and her friends are there."

"So how did you end up halfway across the country?" California was a good ways from Mark's Corners.

"I just moved around for a couple of years, trying to find out what I wanted to do with my life. Being a firefighter kind of fell in my lap, and I was good at it."

"What did you mean when you said you only show people what's on the surface?"

"No one knows about my father, what I did before I moved here. They don't know I don't need to work a day in my life if I didn't want to."

Well hell. That was impressive. "But yet you still work."

"Living the spoiled rich kid life isn't my style. While I've always had money, I always worked hard for it."

"So you live the life of a firefighter while sitting on stacks of money at night."

He threw his head back and laughed. "Not exactly, sweetheart, but that is funny to picture."

"You look like Uncle Scrooge in my head. Diving into your piles of money."

He shook his head, and pushed back his plate. "Now there's a picture. Perhaps you'll need to come over, and see if that's true."

"Maybe." I grabbed our plates, and dumped them in the sink. "I need to make the caramel drizzle for the cake. Did you want to find something to watch?"

"I planned on watching you make that caramel, but I guess I can try to find a movie."

I pointed to the entertainment center. "You should be able to find something in there. Although, I will say that the majority of them are chick flicks."

Abe grimaced. "You trying to put me to sleep?"

I grabbed a saucepan from the cupboard and shook my head. "I'll just cut you a big slice of cake to get you all sugared up."

"I like the sound of that."

Twenty minutes later after Abe moaned and groaned over all of the movies, he finally settled on watching *Overboard.*

"I have to say I'm surprised you settled on a classic." I had all of the Fast and Furious movies, and figured he would have picked one of those. While they weren't chick flicks, they had an over abundance of eye candy which automatically made them chick movies.

I handed him the huge slice of cake drenched in caramel. "Damn, sweetheart. Did you save any for yourself?" I did a bit more than a drizzle on his piece.

It was a pretty big slice. Abe had a quarter of the bundt sitting on his plate, and I had a piece a quarter of his size. "If I ate that much cake you would have to roll me through the door."

He sat back on the couch, kicked up his feet on the coffee table, and forked a huge bit into his mouth. "I'm not a religious man, sweetheart, but this cake has got me wanting to pray to God that you make me cake for the rest of my life."

"You're crazy, Abe."

The movie started playing, and I sat next to him on the couch. He was much to into his cake to notice anything but his fork. Somehow he managed to eat his huge piece of cake before I finished mine, and he set his plate on the coffee table. He looked over at me and smiled. "You have a hell of a lot more control than I do."

"I'm surrounded by it daily. It's a miracle I can look at a cake anymore without hating it." I set my plate down and tried to watch the movie. I could tell Abe was staring at me out of the corner of my eye. "Um, is something wrong?"

"Yeah."

Uh oh. "And that is?"

"You're way too far away from me."

I looked down at the two feet between us. "Really?"

"Yeah, really, sweetheart." He pulled me to him, laid down with his back to the couch, and left me no choice but to lay down next to him. "Much better," he rumbled.

My head was resting on his outstretched arm, and I was laying on my side facing the TV. "What just happened?"

He stuffed a pillow under his head and draped an arm across my middle. "We got comfortable."

I didn't know what to do. I was stretched out on my couch with a gorgeous man who actually wanted to be there with me. "Abe, I don't … is this…"

"Shush, Brynn. Watch the movie and try not to think too hard."

I closed my eyes and sighed. He didn't really give me much chance to do anything but that. After I counted to ten, I opened my eyes to watch Goldie Hawn fall overboard, and fell asleep in Abe's arms.

*

Abe

"Wake up, sweetheart."

She stirred in my arms, and turned to look up at me.

It was half past eleven, and Brynn had passed out in my arms a half an hour into the movie.

"Hey," she rasped. "What time is it?"

"Almost twelve."

She sighed and closed her eyes. "Gah, I have to be up in three hours."

Damn, that sucked. I worked around the clock when I was on shift, but I did tend to get decent sleep as long as there weren't multiple calls in the middle of the night. "Let's get you in bed so you don't wake up with a kink in your neck."

She snuggled into me. "Good here."

"Babe, you should-."

She reached up and pressed a finger to my lips. "Shh. I need to sleep." She relaxed into my arms, and was sleeping again in thirty seconds.

Now that was impressive. Being a firefighter we had all learned to sleep when we could, but Brynn just put us all to shame.

I grabbed the blanket off the back of the couch, draped it over us, and managed to snag the remote she had tucked by her side.

Who was I to argue with a sleeping woman?

She slept, and I enjoyed the feel of her body next to mine.

*

Chapter 5

Brynn

"Wait a minute. He spent the night?" Karen's jaw dropped. "And he's still up there?" She pointed to the ceiling above her.

"Um, yeah." At least I figured he was. I hadn't heard anyone moving around upstairs, and he hadn't walked out the door.

"Damn, girl. Even I sent Blake home at one last night." She packed up the last order of cookies for the day, and stacked the two boxes by the swinging door to the front. "So what are you going to do with him up there?"

"You act like I'm keeping the man captive! I woke up at three, managed to free myself from his hold, and came down here to work. I wasn't going to kick him out at that time of the morning." I grabbed two sprinkled donuts and a cheese danish.

"And just where do you think you're going with those?" she nodded at the pastries in my hand.

"I thought I would take breakfast up to him while I wait for the bread to rise."

Karen smirked. "Try not to get tangled up with him for too long." The bell dinged up front. "You better come back with details, woman." She pushed through the swinging doors, and shouted a greeting to the customer out front.

I tossed my apron on the counter, and slowly climbed the stairs. I could have woken him up when I got up, but I liked him laying my couch. He looked like he belonged there.

My head was in my own thoughts when I opened the door at the top of the stairs and came face to face with Abe shirtless in my kitchen.

Holy hell.

Not what I had expected to see when I opened the door, but I wasn't going to complain.

"Morning, sweetheart."

I choked on my words. "Mor … morning."

"I helped myself to a shower. I hope that's okay? You know that kink I warned you about last night? Well, I woke up with one instead."

My tongue was stuck to the roof of my mouth, and all I could do was stare at his chiseled chest. It was like the man was made out of marble with his perfectly defined abs and all the other delicious small valleys and hills of his ripped body. My eyes traveled lower, and I lost all brain function.

The perfect 'v' into his jeans where the top button was undone did me in.

"You okay?"

I managed to rip my eyes off his body, and looked him in the eye. Not much better to help me regain speech. Now I was lost in his green eyes. "V." Kill me now. My brain was still stuck on the perfect 'v' that invited me to finish unbuttoning his pants and discover just where that 'v' pointed.

"Sweetheart, you can't look at me like that right now."

I blinked slowly. "Huh?"

"You're devouring me with your eyes."

Couldn't get anything past him. "Shirt." I was rendered to one word sentences. They made sense to me, but all Abe did was laugh.

"You want me to put a shirt on, or take yours off?"

Wait, what?

He stalked toward me, and grabbed the pastries from my hand. He tossed them on the table, and pulled me into the living room. "I'll eat those later. Right now there's something I need to do," he mumbled.

He fell back onto the couch, and pulled me down on top of him. I straddled his waist, and splayed my hands on his bare chest. "Wow."

"Not gonna lie, sweetheart. You looking at me, and appreciating all the hard work I put in at the gym makes it all worth it."

My hands roamed over his chest, feeling his soft skin yet hard sculpted body was something I had never felt before. I could sit here for hours and not get tired of touching him.

His hands went to the hem of my shirt, and his eyes connected with mine. "I know you gotta get back to work, but I need to know if you taste as sweet as you look."

I raised my hands over my head, and pulled my shirt off. His hand instantly went to my bra clad breast and squeezed. A low growl ripped from his lips as he pulled one of the cups down, and moved his thumb over my nipple.

I hadn't even kissed the man yet, and he had his hand on my breast. This was so backward, but it felt so good. "Abe?"

"Yeah, sweetheart." His eyes didn't leave my chest.

"Can you kiss me?" So bold, but I couldn't go another second without kissing him.

He delved his fingers into my hair, and pulled my head down. His lips connected with mine, and everything fell into place. My hands continued to roam over his body, and his hand palmed my breast, squeezing and kneading.

I had found heaven in Abe's arms.

*

Abe

Nothing had ever been like this before.

I had never felt the need to give up everything I had just to have another second with a woman. Brynn was all that and more. She could bring a grown man to his knees and beg for mercy.

Her taste on my lips, and her warm, lush breast in my hand was all I ever needed.

"Abe," she gasped against my lips. "How?"

"How what, gorgeous?"

"How are you doing this to me?" she whispered.

"I think I could ask you the same thing, sweetheart."

She wrapped her arms around my neck, and her fingers delved into my hair. "I really need to get back downstairs, but I don't want to."

"Then don't." My lips claimed hers again. Soft, responsive, yielding. She was giving it all to me.

I wrapped my arms around her, and twisted us onto the couch. Her body was laid out beneath me, and she raised her arms over her head.

My fingers pushed her bra up, exposing both of her full breasts, and my breath caught. Perfection was laying beneath me, and I didn't know where to touch her first. My body was on fire for her, and she was fanning the flames with her sweet, seductive innocence.

"Brynn!"

My fingers teased her pert nipples, and her head fell back with a moan falling from her lips.

"Brynn!"

I heard Karen calling for Brynn, but Brynn was in her own world.

"Abe," she gasped.

I leaned down, my lips enveloping her nipple, and my tongue teased the tight bud.

My brain registered the sound of feet pounding up the stairs. Shit. Apparently Karen wasn't going to be ignored.

I quickly pulled Brynn's bra over her breasts, pulled the blanket off the back of the couch, and draped it over her. Her eyes were half-mast, and she looked up at me. "What?"

"One minute, sweetheart." I jumped off the couch, sprinted to the door, and threw it open to Karen with her fist raised.

"'Sup?"

Her eyes bugged out, and she looked down at the floor. "Uh, I need Brynn. Her timer is going off, and I have a cake question for her."

"She ran to the bathroom quick. I'll tell her you need her."

She looked up with a smirk on her face. "You can have her back at four, sparky." She jogged back down the stairs and I shook my head.

"Like I haven't been called that a million times before," I called after her.

She raised her hand over her head, and flipped me off. "Save the hanky panky for later."

I shut the door, and caught a glimpse of Brynn running down the short hallway, and slamming the door to the bathroom behind her.

"Sweetheart, you good?"

She shouted something, but I couldn't make out what she had said. I grabbed my shirt off the back of the kitchen chair, and leaned against the wall by the bathroom. "What's that?"

She wrenched the door open, and pulled her shirt over her head. "That was close. I feel like a sixteen year old getting caught by her parents making out with her boyfriend."

Here I thought she would be freaking out. "We didn't get caught."

"Abe," she laughed, "You answered the door without your shirt on."

I shrugged, and flexed an arm. "Are you complaining?"

She rolled her eyes, and fixed her ponytail. "No, I'm not, but maybe next time put a shirt on when you answer the door to my best friend."

"All I heard was next time." I grabbed her around the waist and buried my face in her neck. Her arms were up in her hair, so she was helpless to push me away. I tracked kisses up her neck and she giggled under my touch.

"Abe, we can't do this right now."

"Then when can we?" I mumbled against her soft skin.

"After I finish work."

"It's only nine. I gotta wait seven hours?"

She lowered her arms, and wrapped them around my neck. "Yes."

"Damn. I guess I could go home and change clothes, run some errands." I leaned back and looked down at her.

She patted me on the shoulder. "Good, you enjoy your day off, and I need to get back to my bread and cakes. You are way too much of a distraction."

"You make that sound like a bad thing, sweetheart."

A laugh bubbled from her lips. "It's only a bad thing when I should be working."

I pressed a kiss to her lips, and rested my forehead against hers. "Then get back to work, and I'll be back around four to continue distracting you."

"I'll be here," she whispered.

"Get to work, sweetheart, before I say fuck it and take you right here."

She jumped away, and wagged her finger at me. "Oh no you don't. You do that, and I'll take those pastries back down with me, and you'll have to forge for your own breakfast."

I held up my hands, and took a huge step back. "Have a good day. I'll see you later."

She laughed and bustled past me. "You're a sucker for baked goods, aren't you, Abe?"

"It's like my kryptonite."

She opened the door, and looked over her shoulder at me. "In that case, have a good day, Superman, and I promise to have a delicious surprise for you tonight."

Well hell.

The door closed behind her, and I tossed my shirt up in the air. I grabbed it mid-air, and pumped my fist.

Fuck yeah.

Tonight was going to be a damn good night.

*

Chapter 6

Brynn

"You never would have came back down if I hadn't walked up those stairs, would you?"

I finished piping the border on the last special order cake for the day, and tossed the piping bag on the counter. "Not true." *Totally true.* I would have stayed up there with Abe until we ran out of food and water.

"Girl, don't lie to me. I saw that man without his shirt on. You'd be a damn fool if you didn't lose all thought when he touched you."

I pointed my spatula at her. "Get out of my head."

She laughed and grabbed the cake from my stand. "I'm in the same boat as you. If Blake were to walk through that door right now and crook his finger at me you'd be left to man the counter alone again."

"You better not leave me alone again." Granted the last time she left me I had met Abe, but I really wasn't into meeting any other hot firefighters. Abe was more than enough for me.

She laughed and placed the cake in the box. "No plans of that, bossman. Besides, if Blake walked in, we would just go check out the storage room for a bit." She wiggled her eyebrows. "I'd just take a fifteen minute break."

She ducked through the swinging doors with the cake in her hands. I tossed my towel at her, but it hit the wall. "No more breaks for you," I called.

By the time three thirty rolled around, Karen was gone, and I was finishing the prep for tomorrow morning. On Sunday's we were only open for four hours, but those four hours were filled with tons of donuts and pastries flying out the door for breakfast and brunches.

A knock sounded on the front door, and I peeked my head out to see Abe standing there with a duffle bag, grocery bags, and a bouquet of roses.

"You're early," I laughed as I opened the door.

"You have no idea how hard it was to stay away this long." He tossed his duffle bag on the floor, handed me the flowers, and dropped the grocery bags at his feet. "I don't know what you did to me, sweetheart, but I missed you more than anything in my life."

His hands delved into my hair, and he kissed me before I could get a word in. His kisses stole my breath and left me panting with need.

"Wow." Rendered speechless yet again. I closed my eyes and sighed.

"You ready to pick up where we left off before?"

I laughed and shook my head. "I still have a couple of things to do for tomorrow. You can either find a vase for these flowers, or watch me work."

He grabbed the flowers and tossed them on the counter. "I've been away from you for too long today, maybe you can teach me a thing or two."

"Maybe you should learn how to fry an egg before you learn how to make a danish."

He grabbed the grocery bags off the floor. "I just gotta put some stuff in the fridge, and then I'll be back down."

He pressed a kiss to my cheek, and jogged up the stairs to my apartment.

I managed to roll and turn the danish dough one last time before Abe came back downstairs.

"Oh man, I missed the good stuff."

I looked up from the slab of dough I had just wrapped up, and my jaw dropped. "Uh, what happened to your shirt?" Abe was standing in my kitchen with no shirt on surrounded by cookies and cakes, but he was the most delicious thing in the place.

"You said we could pick up where we left off before."

I tore my eyes off his ripped chest. "I think I'm done preparing for the day." I actually still had two icings I needed to make, but I could wake up a half an hour earlier, and take care of it the morning.

Abe smirked, and walked through the swinging doors to the front.

"What are you doing?" I called.

He walked back through the doors holding a strawberry confetti cake. "It's time for dessert, sweetheart."

He grabbed my hand, and pulled me up the stairs. "You're insane," I laughed. "What are you going to do with that whole cake?"

"Fuel, sweetheart. We're going to need it later, and I don't want to have to leave the bed to go get it."

My cheeks flushed at his words. "I could always make us a sandwich."

He pushed open the door at the top of the stairs, and beelined through the apartment straight to my bedroom. "You have a good day today?" He set the cake on my bedside table, and his hands went to the button of his jeans.

Uh, what was the question?

He dropped his pants to the floor, and my jaw dropped. The man wasn't wearing underwear.

None.

Zip.

Zilch.

Abe was naked as the day he was born with his rock hard dick pointing straight at me.

"See something you like, sweetheart?"

I ripped my eyes off his dick. "What are you doing?"

"About to fuck you into next week."

Sweet heavens above. "Uh, okay?" I didn't move. Hell, I was amazed that I hadn't passed out when he dropped his pants.

Abe stalked toward me, and my eyes dropped to his bobbing dick. *Whoa.*

His hands went to the hem of my shirt, and he pulled it over my head. He sailed it over his head, and wrapped his arms around me. His fingers deftly unhooked my bra, and pushed it down my arms. "Too many clothes on you, sweetheart."

He didn't need to tell me twice. I unbuttoned my pants, pushing them down along with my underwear. "Better?" I whispered.

He growled low, and lifted me up in his arms. "Much." He buried his face in my breasts, and I gasped as his mouth claimed my nipple. I reached up, pulling the hair tie out of my hair. My hair cascaded down around us. "Fucking love your hair." He pushed me against the wall, and delved his fingers into my hair. "Fucking love everything about you."

Now that sounded nice.

"Been dreaming about what your body would feel like under mine. Perfect tits, lush ass, and skin so soft I want to drown in you and never come up for air."

Lord. Have. Mercy.

"Take me, Abe. Please," I gasped. I had never wanted anything more in my life. Abe was all I could see.

"Feet on the floor," he ordered.

I slowly slipped my legs from around him, and shakily stood.

"Stay right there." He pressed a kiss to my neck. "Stay."

He slowly sunk down to knees trailing kisses down my body the whole way. His warm breath washed over my skin, and he pressed a kiss to my belly button.

I knew what he was going to do, but I wasn't prepared. He parted the lips of my pussy, and blew gently. "This is mine."

God damn.

"Yes." Lord have mercy, *yes*.

He buried his face in my pussy and just, whoa. *Hold the hell on, Brynn.*

My hands shot to his shoulders to hold myself up, and I arched my back to push into his mouth. I moaned with each nip, lick, and twirl of his tongue. Thirty seconds with his face buried in my pussy, and I was ready to come all over his tongue.

"Abe, please." I didn't know if he wanted me to come or not, but in ten more seconds it wasn't going to be left up to him.

He shot up to his feet, his arms lifting me up. "Coming around my dick the first time, sweetheart."

I slid down his body, his dick lined up with my pussy, and I sunk down slowly. He pressed me against the wall, my legs wrapped around his waist, with his dick buried deep inside me. "You ready for this?" he growled into my ear.

So ready. I nodded my head, and pressed a kiss to his lips. "Yes, please."

He slowly pulled out, then plunged back in. "So fucking sweet," he murmured. He buried his face in my hair, and I wrapped my arms around his neck.

"Yes," I hissed. He thrusted in and out, driving me close to the edge. "I need you, Abe." Damn, did I crave him. More than I needed my next breath.

"You come for me, sweetheart. For me only." He pushed off the wall, and stalked to the bed. He laid me down, his dick buried inside me. My ass was on the edge of the bed, and he stood over me. He put his hands on the back of my knees, and pushed my legs open. "You ready for this? Once I come inside you, there's no going back. You're mine, Brynn."

Primitive.

Territorial.

Demanding.

All for me.

I bit my lip. "Yes," I whispered.

He thrusted hard, and my eyes rolled back in my head. And this was how it was done. Abe took my body, and worshipped it. His hands roamed over my breasts, while his dick drilled into me.

"Yes, yes," I moaned. My orgasm built with each thrust until I slammed my eyes shut, and stars exploded behind my eyelids.

Abe's guttural moans surrounded me as he thrust deep, and filled my spasming pussy with his come

He collapsed on top of me, his breathing short and labored. "Mine," he gasped.

I was good with that, because he was mine also.

*

Abe

"Don't get crumbs in my bed."

I shoveled a forkful of moist cake into my mouth. God damn, Brynn could bake. "This cake is too good to drop any crumbs, sweetheart." I held up a bite to her.

She wrapped her lips around the fork, and moaned. "I do make good cake," she giggled.

"The best."

Brynn and I had spent the rest of the day in bed learning and discovering each other.

"When do you go back to work?"

"Monday morning, eight am."

She laid her head on my shoulder, and drew circles on my stomach with her fingertip. "Hmm."

"What's wrong, sweetheart?"

"Nothing. It's just going to suck to have to go that many days without seeing you."

I finished a quarter of the cake and set the rest back on the nightstand. "You'll still see me. Maybe not as much, but I know the guys would appreciate fresh donuts and cake everyday."

She tilted her head back and looked up at me. "I'm pretty sure if I brought donuts everyday you guys would always be in the gym and not out fighting fires and rescuing kittens from trees."

"Then we'll have to find another reason for you to stop by the station." Captain was going to have to deal with Brynn being there during downtime if he expected me to not be a grumpy asshole.

She sighed and laid her head back down. "We'll figure it out I guess." She giggled, and resumed drawing lazy circles on my stomach. "I think I'm going to need something more than cake for sustenance."

"I think you need an Abe special." I rolled out from under her, and slid out of bed.

"An Abe special? I'm kind of afraid of what that might be since I know you can't cook."

I left her in the bed and walked to the fridge. "Trust me, Brynn. I'll never steer you wrong," I called. After I popped one of the containers I had brought over into the microwave, I grabbed a fork from the drawer, and grabbed the chilled bottle of wine.

I hadn't planned on surviving on only cake tonight. I had planned on spending the night in bed with Brynn, and brought the perfect food to help us keep up our stamina.

Chicken Alfredo from Mario's was just what we needed right now.

I filled two wine glasses, grabbed the steaming container from the microwave, and hightailed it back to the bedroom.

"Ah, the Abe Special is having someone else cook," she laughed. She sat up and draped the blanket over her shoulders. "I guess I can handle that."

I handed her a glass of wine, and managed to crawl into bed without spilling any wine or food. "I'm a work in progress, sweetheart."

"I wouldn't say that." She grabbed the container and stirred the sauce laden noodles around. "How did you know Chicken Alfredo was my favorite?"

"I may or may not have talked to Karen on the way out today. She gave me a little insight into Brynn Marshall."

"Is that so? I might have to ask her where her loyalty lies."

She loaded the fork with pasta and chicken, and held it up to my lips. "She's loyal to you, sweetheart. I just happened to have Blake's number that she was jonesing to have."

"Typical," she muttered.

For every bite she took, she fed me three.

"You ready for round three?" I asked as she ate the last bite.

She set the plate on the floor, and shook her head. "I'm pretty sure this is going to be round five."

Shit, really? I grabbed her around the waist, and pulled her to my side. "Well, whatever number it is, I'm ready for more."

"You're rather insatiable."

"Only when it comes to you, sweetheart."

"And cake," she sassed.

I rolled my eyes, and pressed a kiss to her cheek. "But only your cake."

"Pretty sure that's a double entendre."

I wiggled my eyebrows. "That's because both types of your cake are so sweet."

Her cheeks heated and she blushed ten shades of red.

"There's the sweet innocence that caught my attention that first day."

Brynn

"Wanna know what caught my attention the first time I saw you?" I asked.

"Tell me, sweetheart."

I brushed my fingertips across his cheek. "I don't know how to say this," I muttered.

"You can tell me anything."

I sighed, and a grin spread across my lips. "That you picked the right profession because you are smokin' hot."

He busted out laughing, and rested her forehead on mine. "I don't know what I'm gonna do with you."

I shrugged. "At least I'll keep you on your toes."

"Can I use a cheesy line on you now?" he whispered.

I nodded.

"I've been in more fires in my career than I can count, but I've never been consumed like I am with you. You're the sweetest burn, sweetheart."

My eyes closed and I sighed. "I don't know what to say, Abe."

"Nothing to say. I think it's time to let our bodies do the talking again."

"And then what?" I had known this man for four days. This wasn't something that happened everyday.

"Uh, we eat more cake, and then we see if I can keep you up all night."

I giggled and smacked him on the shoulder. "I meant after tonight."

He pressed a kiss to my cheek and pulled the covers over us. "We keep burning up the sheets, and everything else will work it's way out. You're what I want, Brynn. I know we barely know each other, but sometimes that doesn't matter. Sometimes you just know, and the second I saw you, I knew that you were it."

My hand cupped his cheek and I smiled. "I couldn't have said it better myself."

"Good. Now let's see about setting these sheets on fire."

"And then cake?" I giggled.

"And then cake, sweetheart."

The End

Make sure to pick up
Five Alarm Donuts!
Karen and Blake's story!

About the Author

Winter Travers is a devoted wife, mother, and aunt turned author who was born and raised in Wisconsin. After a brief stint in South Carolina following her heart to chase the man who is now her hubby, they retreated back up North to the changing seasons, and to the place they now call home.

Winter spends her days writing happily ever after's, and her nights zipping around on her forklift at work. She also has an addiction to anything MC related, her dog Thunder, and Mexican food! (Tamales!)

Winter loves to stay connected with her readers. Don't hesitate to reach out and contact her.

http://www.facebook.com/wintertravers
Twitter: @WinterTravers
Instagram: @WinterTravers
http://www.wintertravers.com/

Coming Soon

Holeshot
Nitro Crew Series
Book 2
September 29th

Made in the USA
Monee, IL
14 February 2025

12287661R00039